D0056328

This fun phonics reader

belongs to

Maya Patel

Contents

Ladybird

Cover illustration by John Haslam

A catalogue record for this book is available from the British Library

Published by Ladybird Books Ltd
27 Wrights Lane London W8 5TZ
A Penguin Company

2 4 6 8 10 9 7 5 3 1

© LADYBIRD BOOKS LTD MM

by Clive Gifford
illustrated by John Haslam

introducing the ck letter group,
as in duck

Stunt Duck gave his jet pack one last check.

He put the jet pack on his back and locked the straps.

"Stand back,"
said Stunt Duck.

Click! He lit his jet pack with a quick flick.

Stunt Duck shot into the bricks and blocks.

Smack! He struck the rock at the back.

Crack! Stunt Duck hit the deck. It all went black.

"Nice trick, Stunt Duck,
but the film got stuck.
Can you do it again?"

11

Bad luck, Stunt Duck!

Roll up!
Roll up!

by Clive Gifford
illustrated by Charlotte Combe

introducing the **ll** and **ss**
letter groups, as in we**ll** and mi**ss**

We all had a ball when
the fair came to call.

Roll Up! Roll Up!

Nell did well
on all the stalls.

15

Bess won less, but still did well.

Ring the bell to win a doll.

Win a Doll

17

The Hall of Chills was full of thrills.

19

I went wild on the Wacky Wall.

Wacky Wall

Don't fall, Bill!

Bess got in a mess with her candy floss.

Mum will be cross.

And we sat on the hill as evening fell.

This is bliss!

The Sing Song Gang

by Clive Gifford
illustrated by Eric Smith

introducing the `ng` sound,
as in ki`ng`

DING DONG!
BANG BANG BANG!

24

"Hang on!" said the King,
as the door bell rang.

"Open up!
It's the Sing Song Gang!

Would you like us to sing
as you swing on your swing?

You can bang on the gong,

CLANG

BONG

or play one of the strings."

TWANG

PING

So the gang sang a song,

and the King sang along.

31

phonics

Learn to read with Ladybird

phonics is one strand of Ladybird's **Learn to Read** range. It can be used alongside any other reading programme, and is an ideal way to support the reading work that your child is doing, or about to do, in school.

This chart will help you to pick the right book for your child from Ladybird's three main **Learn to Read** series.

Age	Stage	Phonics	Read with Ladybird	Read it yourself
4-5 years	Starter reader	Books 1-3	Level 1	Level 1
5-6 years	Developing reader	Books 2-9	Level 1-2	Level 2-3
6-7 years	Improving reader	Books 10-12	Level 2-3	Level 3-4
7-8 years	Confident reader		Level 3-4	Level 4

Ladybird has been a leading publisher of reading programmes for the last fifty years. **phonics** combines this experience with the latest research to provide a rapid route to reading success.

Some common words, such as 'one', 'said' and even 'the', can't be read by sounding out. Help your child practise recognising words like these so that he can read them on sight, as whole words.

Phonic fun

Playing word games is a fun way to build phonic skills. Write down a consonant group and see how many words your child can think of beginning or ending with that group. For extra fun, try making up silly sentences together, using some or all of the words.

The du<u>ck</u> in his so<u>ck</u> gave Mi<u>ck</u> a sho<u>ck</u>.

Books in the phonics series

Book 1 **Alphapets**
Introduces the most common sound made by each letter, and the capital and small letter shapes.

Book 2 **Splat cat**
Simple words including the short vowel sounds `a` `e` and `i` as in cat, hen and pig.

Book 3 **Hot fox**
Simple words including the short vowel sounds `o` and `u` ; simple words including `ch` `sh` or `th`

Book 4 **Stunt Duck**
Simple words including the common consonant combinations `ck` `ll` `ss` and `ng`.

Book 5 **Sheriff Showoff**
More words including common consonant blends: `ff` `st` `mp` `lp` `nch` `nd` and `fl`.

Book 6 **Frank's frock**
More words including common consonant blends: `fr` `nk` `cl` `tr` `gr` and `nt`.

Match the sounds ga

36 self-checking phonic gamecards. Great fun, and the i way to practise the spellings and introduced in the phonics st